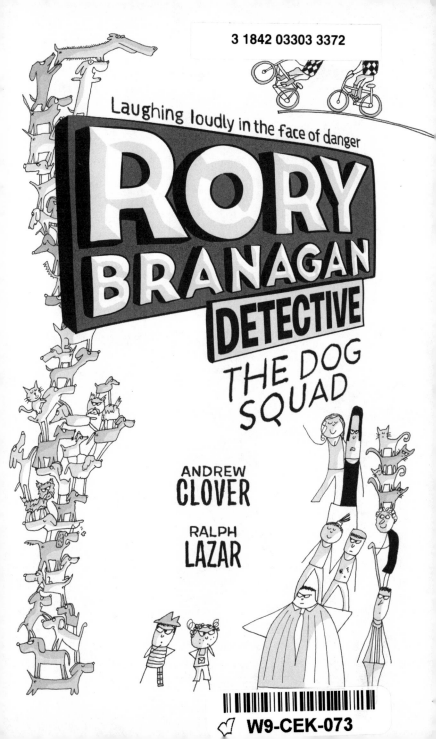

Laughing loudly in the face of danger

# RORY BRANAGAN
## DETECTIVE
### THE DOG SQUAD

ANDREW
**CLOVER**

RALPH
**LAZAR**

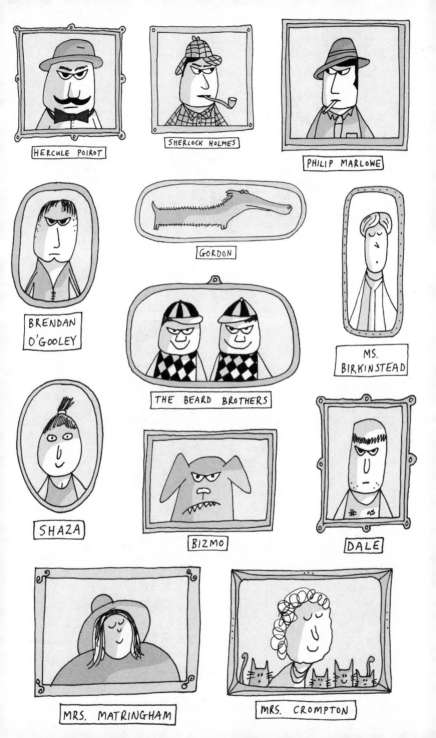

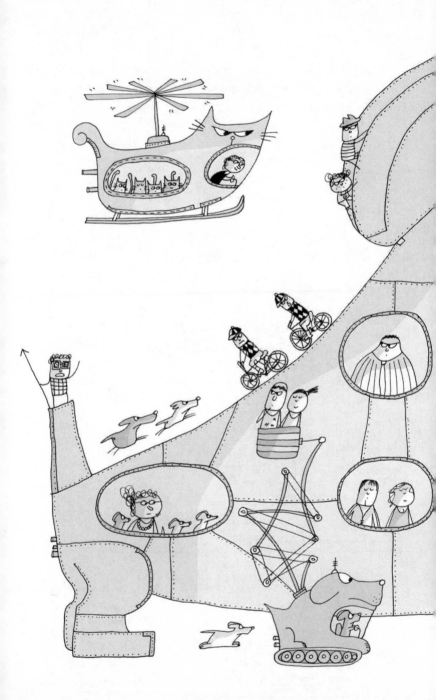

# W

PENGUIN WORKSHOP
An Imprint of Penguin Random House LLC, New York

Text copyright © 2018 by Andrew Clover. Illustrations copyright © 2018
by Ralph Lazar. All rights reserved. First published in Great Britain in 2018 by
HarperCollins Children's Books. Published in the United States in 2020 by
Penguin Workshop, an imprint of Penguin Random House LLC, New York.
PENGUIN and PENGUIN WORKSHOP
are trademarks of Penguin Books Ltd, and
the W colophon is a registered trademark of
Penguin Random House LLC. Printed in the USA.

Visit us online at www.penguinrandomhouse.com.

Library of Congress Cataloging-in-Publication Data is
available upon request.

ISBN 9781524793661          10 9 8 7 6 5 4 3 2 1

We dedicate this to
ALL DOGS EVERYWHERE
(and to the people
who love them)

I am Rory Branagan.

I am actually a detective.

Only three days ago, I, with my new

Best Friend and Accomplice, Cassidy

"the Cat" Callaghan, trailed

some poisoners to the Deadly

Pirate restaurant, where we

*GOT THEM*!!

Soon I am going to be the *Biggest*

*Detective in the World*!!

I am even going to solve the *biggest mystery in my life*, which is: WHERE IS MY DAD?

He disappeared when I was three.

Literally . . .

One moment he was there—cracking jokes, telling stories, and being the *best dad in the world.*

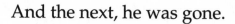

And the next, he was gone.

*BUT THEN...*

Three days ago, I got a *secret letter* from him. He said he was hiding *in the place where he was once happiest.* So now I know he's *alive,* but I'm thinking ...

*Where IS he?*

Is he living in a tree house in a secret island hideout?

I'm thinking ... Where *was he happiest?*

Was it some place far away, where he once went on vacation?

I ask my brother who is *looming*
by the hallway mirror. He got the
first four hairs of his mustache last week,
and now he rushes out, ten times a day, to
see if more have appeared.

"Where do you think Dad is?" I ask.

"I don't know," he says. "I *do* know Mom
gets mad if we even ask."

"OK," I say, "where do you think he was happiest?"

"Why are you even *asking*?" he says.

"Because," I tell him, "I am just . . . being a detective."

# "MOM!!!"

he shouts.

"He's BEING A DETECTIVE AGAIN!"

And, two seconds later, Mom appears,
and already she looks set to *blow up*.

"RORY!"
she says "You are NOT
a detective!"

"I *am*," I reply. "Even the policeman said so when I solved a *crime*."

Now she's more set to explode than a ship with ten *cannons* that are about to go BOOM.

"Rory," she says, "you need to think about OTHER PEOPLE. I am *trying* to keep this family together, and it's *hard enough* without you getting into danger. There are some *bad people* out there. Last time you were being a detective you hurt your leg *very badly*."

Now THAT is a *tiny bit true*, I suppose.

I did sprain my leg very badly, which is why I am supposed to be spending ONE WHOLE WEEK in bed wearing a surgical boot.

"But I did not hurt my leg because of *bad people*," I say, "but because I jumped over a high gate, and landed next to a pig . . ."

And that *does* it. Suddenly my mom . . .

... BLOWS UP like a ship with a *hundred cannons* that are all *BLASTING OFF*.

# "NO!!!

I do *not* want some story!" she screams.

"I just need you to stay in your bed doing your homework, and, if I find you've been being a detective, you will be in the **worst trouble** of your life!"

But even as Mom is shouting I am thinking: *But I LOVE being a detective!* I am thinking: *I even like getting into danger!*

And I swear ... it is literally only about an hour after that ...

. . . that Cat and I discover a *real, actual crime*, and end up getting into the very *DEADLIEST OF DEADLY DANGERS*!!!

I'll tell you the whole story.

## CHAPTER ONE
## A Call to Adventure

It all starts ... with me doing something that is not DANGEROUS at all. I am lying in my room. I am having a cool, *relaxing* time reading a book.

It is about Napoleon.

Apparently he was small but he became the most *powerful person in the world*, and I am thinking . . . *I am small. I could become the most powerful person in the world.*

Suddenly my brother's **big head** appears.

"There is someone at the door for you," he says.

"Who is it?" I ask.

But he just goes.

But I don't mind.

You don't need to be a genius to *detect* that the person coming is Cassidy "the Cat" Callaghan. I can hear her *singing* as she comes up the stairs.

"DUM-DUM-der-dum-dum-DUM!" she sings, then she . . .

*leaps* into the room.

"Hello, *Deadly*!" she says. (That's what she calls me!)

"Hello, Cat!" I reply. (That's what I call her!)

"So," she says, "will we go out to track clues and solve crimes?"

"Er . . . no," I say. "I can't just now . . .
because of my leg!"

"Oh, I won't let you be stopped by
a little thing like that! I have prepared
something!" she says. "Come on! I'll give
you a piggyback ride."

I get on her back and she piggybacks
me out of the room and down the stairs.

"Behold," she says. "Your *chariot*!"

It's a garbage can.

"I am NOT going in there!" I tell her.

"I have *cleaned* it," she says, "and I've put in cushions, and I also have something *very detective-y* to show you!"

So now she's got me *interested*.

"Stand back!" I command. "I shall *mount the chariot*!"

I get in and she rolls me out the door.

"*Charge!*" she shouts, and she starts to *sprint* up the street.

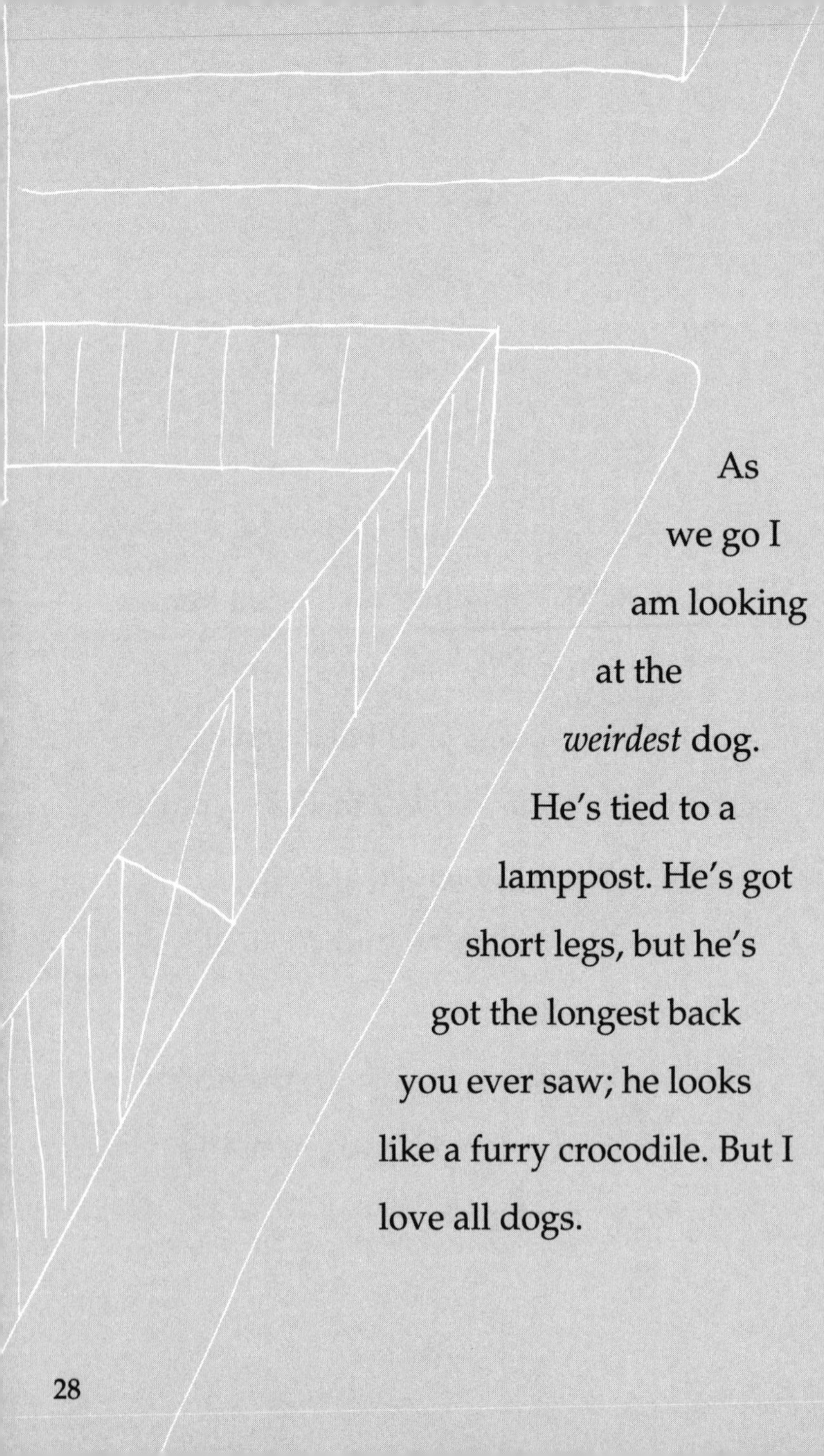

As
we go I
am looking
at the
*weirdest* dog.
He's tied to a
lamppost. He's got
short legs, but he's
got the longest back
you ever saw; he looks
like a furry crocodile. But I
love all dogs.

"Hello,
boy!"
I call.
He wags
his tail, and
you can see he's
friendly. So now
I'm longing to go
back and stroke him.
But the Cat is in the
mood to go fast.

"*Full speed!*" she says.

She *hurtles* all the way to the store where the *detective-y thing* she wants to show me turns out to be a magazine called *Real Detective*, but we haven't actually brought *money* to buy it, and also I can't go into the store in my "chariot."

So we read it by the door. I see right away that *Real Detective* is *great*. We open it to read the cover story.

# REAL DETECTIVE

## SECRETS OF

## THE FAMOUS DETECTIVES

Nº 1

SHERLOCK HOLMES

Secret: Notice

EVERYTHING.

We turn the page. There's ...

# REAL DETECTIVE

## SECRETS OF
## THE FAMOUS DETECTIVES

HERCULE POIROT
Secret: List all
suspects. List
their motives.

Nº3

PHILIP MARLOWE
Secret: Don't be
afraid to *fight*.

I am just thinking that I LOVE this magazine when I . . . Rory Branagan (detective) NOTICE a real, actual crime.

A clue hits me in the face. It's a piece of paper blown by the wind.

It says . . .

"Lost: Ben, our much-loved greyhound dog."

And there's a picture of a dog looking sad.

I then notice on a lamppost . . .

Right away my heart is pounding. I cannot BELIEVE someone is actually TAKING dogs from Dean Swift Drive, which is my *actual street*. I am already very angry, but also very curious.

"Rory," says Cat, "look."

I look, and at the other end of the road *someone is taking the furry crocodile*. They're wearing a black coat and a black wool hat.

"Is that dog ...?" I start.

"Being stolen?" says Cat.

You can tell the crocodile doesn't like it. The thief and dog are turning the corner into Roy Keane Court.

*"Quick!"* I say. "Follow that dog!"

It's two hundred yards but Cat RUNS all the way.

But when we get to Roy Keane Court, there's NO ONE there.

We run down it.

We look left. There's NO ONE.

We look right. There's NO ONE.

We look in the trees. There's NO ONE.

We turn around.

There's Corner Boy, my neighbor.

He's standing on his corner, but he's
staring up at a window on Jay Byrne
Road.

"Corner Boy!" I shout. "Did you just
see a person stealing a dog?"

"No! All I saw was that Jack Russell up there," he says (pointing up to the left). "He always goes WILD if anyone goes past."

"Did he go wild?"

"No."

Cat turns to me. "So," she says, "that means the thief did not go up there."

"Could they be hiding in one of those cars?" I say.

"Good thinking!" says Cat.

She sprints past each of the cars. She looks into all of them, then runs back.

"I saw nothing," she pants. "That means whoever took that dog MUST have gone into one of these five houses!"

I'm thinking: *She could be right!* But I'm also thinking: *But, if she's wrong, then the dog thief could still be OUT and ABOUT and if they are, they MIGHT TAKE WILKINS WELKIN!!!!!*

But some people might not know who Wilkins Welkin is.

I shall explain . . .

## CHAPTER TWO
## Wilkins Welkin, King of Dogs

When my mom goes out she always invites over Mrs. Welkin, the old lady from across the street, and before she leaves she ALWAYS says, "Are you *sure* you'll be OK?"

It's AS IF Mom thinks that as soon as she goes out Mrs. Welkin is *leaping over the wall with a sword . . .*

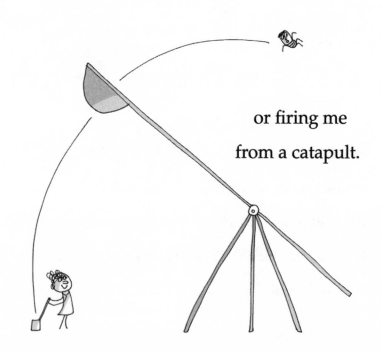

or firing me from a catapult.

I actually *love* it when Mrs. Welkin comes, because she brings Wilkins Welkin, her sausage dog.

You wouldn't know it to see him, but he is *quite a character*.

As soon as he sees me
he goes *BERSERK*—
*leaping* about
and *wagging*
his tail.

Then he lets me rub his tummy.

Then, suddenly, he *starts his tricks*.

First he does two or three commando rolls.

Then he sprints into the living room, then

he LEAPS UP to the windowsill where . . .

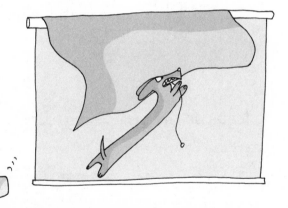

. . . he starts madly yanking on the

blind, going *rrr-rrr-rrrr*.

(I have no idea why he does that!)

But then suddenly
he leaps off again.

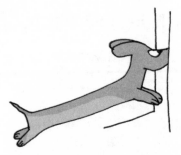

He powers up the stairs ...

He pokes open my
door with his nose ...

He leaps on my bed ...

... and he gets *straight down to business* staring out of the window.

He stares out for ages.

It's as if he knows that if he turns his attention away *for a moment* ...

… in that moment *twenty cats will go by.*

They'll be swinging on the clothesline.

They'll be entering the house.

In no time at all they will be *romping* around everywhere, *scratching* and leaving *fur* and their evil catty *stink*.

Wilkins is determined that this will NOT happen. (Not on his watch.) He looks out *for ages*.

I *love* it when he does that. I *love* Wilkins Welkin. And to my horror I realize that as we went running down the street just now, I saw *him in his garden*.

"Quick!" I shout. "Take me back to Mrs. Welkin's!"

Cat dashes down past Corner Boy.
We *shoot* down the middle of the street
toward Mrs. Welkin's.

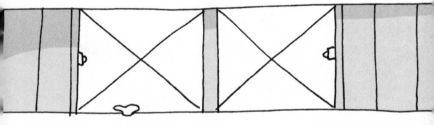

As I look through the gate, I can't see
Wilkins. But then . . .

. . . he appears (looking totally calm).
He's just sniffing a piece of burrito
that someone's dropped by his gate.

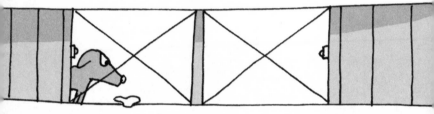

Then he turns. He sees me in the trash-
can chariot, and he thinks I'm trapped. He
gives me a look, as if to say, *"Don't worry,
Rory, I am coming FOR YOU!"* And then
he LAUNCHES himself at the gate.

Cat pushes the chariot toward him, I bend down, Wilkins and I *hug* and for about six seconds I'm *totally happy*.

But then *my mom appears* from Mrs. Welkin's house. She sees me.

She also sees that I am not lying in bed doing homework, but am, in fact, charging up and down the street in a garbage can.

To describe how Mom *reacts* I will first have to tell you about the *Orient*, which was Napoleon's biggest ship . . .

One night a flaming cannonball hit its gunpowder store, and it EXPLODED in a *blast* that *shook the sky* right across Egypt.

That is the kind of blast that happens right now.

As I look up at her, I'm thinking *I could cry, and I don't want to in front of Cassidy.* I also don't want to run home just because Mom is *shouting in the street.*

I turn to Mrs. Welkin, who is behind Mom, and I say, "Mrs. Welkin, I've been getting *lonely* at home . . . could I borrow Wilkins for company?"

She gives me a wise, kind look.

"I'm sure Wilkins would *love* to visit you, Rory," she says.

She lifts him into the chariot. She also gives me his favorite squeaky hedgehog.

"Just make sure he doesn't eat any take-out food," she says. "It gives him gas."

"Oh," I say, "I know that!"

I definitely DO know that. Wilkins eats the food that people drop, and then he does LETHAL FARTS. He does one now. (I can feel it echoing around the trash can.)

"But the main thing is," says Mrs. Welkin, "with this dog thief around, you must watch him at all times!"

"Oh, I will do that!" I promise.

"I know you will," says Mrs. Welkin.

And with that we head off toward home. I don't even mind anymore about Mom shouting. We have Wilkins, and nothing else matters.

As we cross the street we pass Dale and Shaza, who just moved into the apartment at the bottom of our garden. They're all right. But they have a huge, lethal *rottweiler* called Bizmo.

Bizmo thinks it's WEIRD that I'm in the trash can.

He starts to bark. *RUR-RUR-RUR*, he goes, in a deep, bearlike growl, as if he's saying, *"I cannot allow THIS on my street!"*

Wilkins sticks his face over the top of the can. *RRRR-RRRR-RRRR*, he goes, as if to say, *"This is NOT your street. It belongs to ME, and RORY, and MRS. WELKIN!"*

And the trouble is . . . as he does that,
he knocks his hedgehog out of the
chariot.

*RIGHT!* thinks Bizmo (the big greedy
bully), *I will have THAT!* And he picks up
the hedgehog, and walks off with it.

Wilkins is *furious*. He barks, *rur-rur-rur*—as if to say: *"You have taken my hedgehog, and I will TAKE YOU DOWN, Bizmo. I will TAKE YOU DOWN!"*

Dale and Shaza walk off. Wilkins runs up my chest, leaps, and then SOARS INTO THE SKY like he's SUPERDOG . . .

He is *flying* down toward Bizmo— teeth ready to bite, BUT unfortunately *as he does* . . .

*Brendan O'Gooley* is crossing the street past Bizmo. Brendan is the biggest, toughest *knucklehead* around. He *catches* Wilkins and squeezes him in his meaty hands.

*"Don't you touch our dog!"* I shout.

"You stop your dog barking," he says, "or *I* will!"

And he *dunks* Wilkins into the chariot.

*"I don't want to hear another dog barking EVER AGAIN!"* he growls.

Brendan strides off up the street.

And, staring after him, I say to the Cat, "Did you hear him? He said he didn't want to hear *any* dogs *ever again*. He practically ADMITTED he's taking the dogs, and I say he's an evil, ignorant scumbag, and I say we *BRING HIM DOWN!!*"

She gives me one of her most catty looks.

"Don't you think you're being a bit *prejudiced*?" she says.

I say, "HUH!"

# CHAPTER THREE
## A Quick Word about Prejudice

Our head teacher, Ms. Birkinstead, is always giving lectures about prejudice, which is when you judge someone on how they look, which, she says, is very, very bad.

"You don't judge a book by its cover," she says.

Which I always think is NOT TRUE.

I *always* judge a book by its cover—e.g., if it is called *Fun with Tractors*, and it has a picture of a *tractor* . . .

. . . I don't read it.

Or, if the book is called *Ten Little Unicorns*, or *Ten Little ANYTHING*, I *definitely* don't read it, because in those books the SAME THING always happens.

First there are ten little unicorns
trotting out to play (clip-clop, clip-clop).

But then one trots away.

Then there are nine little unicorns
trotting out to play (clip-clop, clip-clop).

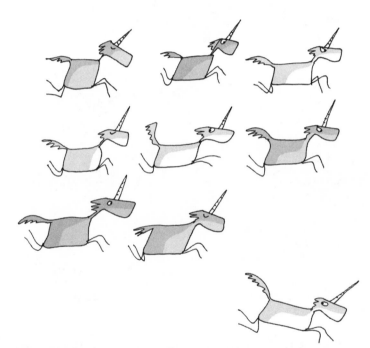

But then another trots away.

Then there are eight little unicorns
trotting out to play (clip-clop, clip-clop).

And by the time there are *seven* little
unicorns (trotting out to play) you are
wishing you could . . .

*. . . crush all the unicorns with a big hammer.*

You want all unicorns to trot *down
a toilet*, and you want them to be
FLUSHED out over a swamp.

SPLASH!

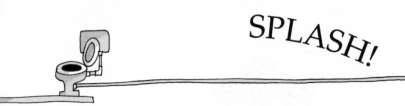

All right, *OK* . . . I know you should not

judge everyone just on their face.

But the reason I am judging Brendan O'Gooley is because he just *shoved his face* into mine, and then said, "I don't want to hear another dog barking ever again!" Plus he has blond, greasy hair parted in the center, so his head looks like a BUTT.

"I am not saying that Brendan DEFINITELY is a bad guy, who is

stealing all the dogs," I say to Cat. "But I am *definitely* saying he looks like a big BUTTHEAD, and I *suspect* him."

"Fair enough," she says. "But you'd better get EVIDENCE before you accuse him."

She now pushes me into my house. I climb out of the chariot.

"I can see his apartment from my window," I tell her. "I'll watch it!"

"You do that!" she says.

"Don't you want to spy on him with me?" I ask.

"I don't think your mom is that keen on me just now," she says. "So I'd better go home."

And she does.

Wilkins leaves too. He doesn't even bother going to the living room to pull the blind. He just *shoots* up the stairs.

By the time I get into the room he's already in position.

He is looking out, like the captain of an old-style ship staring at the horizon.

"Captain Wilkins," I say, "do you mind if I join you?"

He shuffles over to make room. He then looks out of the window. *I* look out of the window.

And THAT is how the Great Stakeout starts.

CHAPTER FOUR
The Great Stakeout

By the way, *the Great Stakeout* is
NOT a great juicy steak that gets left
out. A stakeout is when detectives
watch something or someone, to
gather EVIDENCE.

The first thing that happens—at 12:52 p.m.—is we see Mrs. Crompton's cats come into *our* garden. They scratch their claws on our tree house tree. Wilkins goes *rrrrrr*.

Then I look into the bathroom window of my archenemy Michael Beard, who lives three doors down. He is dancing around in his underpants looking like an idiot. I laugh. That's at 12:54 p.m.

Then at 1:06 p.m., I see Dale and Shaza coming back. He is holding a black coat. I remember the dog thief had a black coat. *Interesting*, I'm thinking. *Very, very interesting*.

Then I see Brendan "the Butthead"
O'Gooley leaving the house. He is quite
literally HOLDING A DOG CAGE!!
*He is so obviously the*
*thief!* Why does
no one STOP him?

Then we see nothing for quite a
while. (And that includes my so-called
Accomplice, Cassidy. I'm thinking: *Where*
*the HECK is she?*)

Then—at 2:06 p.m.—she
comes out of her house.
She jumps up on her wall,
and she just stands there,
looking like a tightrope
walker.

And about one second after that, Rupert Beard (Michael Beard's even more annoying brother) goes by. The Beards both want to be jockeys. They're both tiny, and they're such *show-offs*. Rupert Beard is on a bike—making it rear up like a horse and he's fully dressed—*head to foot*—in brand-new jockey clothes.

"Hey, Catty-Cat Callaghan!" he calls. "Do you like my new bike?"

"Yes," says Cassidy. "And I like your hat!"

"Have it!" he says, and Frisbees it *at her*. So now *cannonballs* are booming in my head. I'm thinking: *How come he's got so much money that he's got a new bike and he's giving out hats?* I'm thinking: *Cat Callaghan is MY name for her!* (*How come* HE's *using it?*)

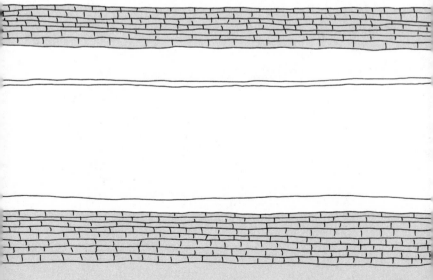

But then, as Rupert Beard swoops
round the corner into Jay Byrne Road
(still on one wheel), someone is coming
the other way, and it is . . .

Mrs. Matringham, the "Dog Lady."

She is an *enormous* woman, who has a pack of SIX dogs. She LOVES them. She has named them all after celebrities.

Her last two (short-haired Yorkshire terriers) are Nicki Minaj and Ed Sheeran.

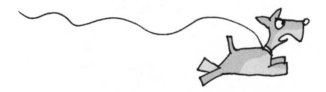

Ed Sheeran is a little ginger dog. He's got beady eyes. He can see a cat across the street, and he *charges out*.

Rupert Beard has to swerve.

But prime suspect Brendan O'Gooley
is just arriving in his van and Beard
*smacks into the side.*

Brendan slams on his brakes, and
leaps out. Everyone SCRAMBLES. I can't
believe it. He clears the street in one
second.

"I don't know what YOU'RE looking
at!" he screams, suddenly turning to *me*.

TERRIFIED, I shut the window so fast I bop Wilkins on his nose. He does a fart that smells of garlic, then falls to the floor.

I've shut the window just in time. Two seconds later, Mom comes in.

"Rory Branagan," she says, "what *are* you doing?"

I play it cool. "Oh," I say, "I've just been reading about Napoleon."

I pat the book, as if we're old friends.

"Have you?" says Mom.

"Yes," I tell her. "Cover to cover."

Mom shows me a page for about 0.4 seconds.

"So what was that part about?" she asks.

"It's about Napoleon's tactics in battle," I tell her.

"Go on then," she says. "Tell me about his tactics in battle."

"Well," I say (and I'm trying to remember), "there is Attack from the Flanks (when Napoleon would attack from the flanks). And there is Looting and Pillaging (when he would take the enemies' stuff). And there's Guerrilla Attacks, which is when he would send in gorillas (because sometimes he'd come to a big castle, and soldiers couldn't get in, but gorillas could, or even monkeys) . . ."

## "Send in the **monkeys!**"

103

"RORY!" shouts Mom. "It's 'Guerrilla Attack,' not 'Gorilla Attack.' That is where troops *hide* and then they leap out and *fight*, and then they *hide* again. Don't just make things up: you need to *understand*! Your imagination will get you into a lot of trouble one of these days!"

With that, she pulls the curtains SHUT.

"And if I find out you've been doing anymore staring out of that window," she says, "it'll be boarded up."

## CHAPTER FIVE
## Paperwork

After that my mom's lurking around.

*I'd better not look out of that window to do any detecting,* I think. So I decide to do all my paperwork.

I think this could actually be my favorite thing about being a detective: I get out all my pens and rulers and draw a map of my area, marking up all the places of IMPORTANCE to the CRIME.

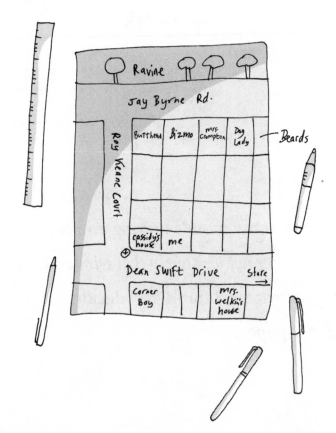

And after I have done that, I draw a diagram of the *five* suspects' houses, and I write their names . . .

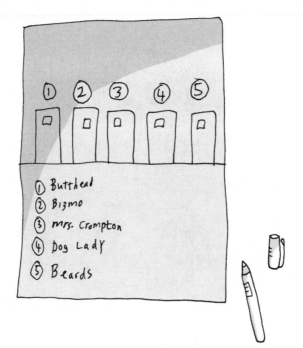

After that I write up any *evidence* I've found.

Brendan O'Gooley (PRIME SUSPECT/THE BIG BUTTHEAD) lives in the house on the corner in the downstairs apartment.

The top apartment is to let. I know this because there is a sign outside, which Corner Boy has changed so that it says . . .

At the house next door, the top apartment is for sale. I know this because there is a sign, which Corner Boy has changed so it reads . . .

Underneath that are Dale, Shaza, and Bizmo. I realize they also have a van—like Brendan (useful for transporting stolen dogs).

But I also realize that it would be almost impossible for them to be handling the dogs with Bizmo around, because he'd be trying to fight them, and I *conclude* that for that reason . . .

. . . THEY ARE NOT LIKELY TO BE THE THIEVES.

Next door there is just Mrs. Crompton. She owns the whole house. I think she also is very, very unlikely to be stealing dogs. She's 102, and she lives with four cats.

VERY, VERY UNLIKELY TO BE THE THIEF.

Next door to her is the Dog Lady.

POSSIBLE MOTIVE: SHE WANTS TO OWN ALL THE DOGS IN THE WORLD.

Next to her is the house of Michael Beard, Rupert Beard, and Mrs. Beard (their mom). I am thinking, *I can easily imagine they* might *be taking dogs*. But I cannot think WHY.

Then someone comes in.

It's Corner Boy holding a plate of food.

"I've made some cookies," he says.

(They look *disgusting*. I swear he's put *maggots* in them!) "I'm raising money for my dad, because he's still in the hospital."

"Oh, right!" I say, and I buy all of them.

I tell Corner Boy I think Brendan O'Gooley is the dog thief.

"He's probably selling them," says Corner Boy. "Rich people buy them. They stuff them and put them on the wall, and they make wallets out of their ears, and they have the tails sticking out of the walls for when they want to turn on the lights."

I am trying to picture that.

"I can't believe that!" I say.

"It's true," he replies. "My mom read it in the paper."

Then he goes.

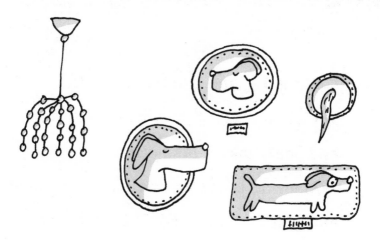

*But wait one moment,* I think as he clumps down the stairs. *If someone is stealing dogs for money, then I bet it's the Beards. They've definitely got loads of cash all of a sudden.*

I decide I have to spy on them again. That's at 5:43 p.m.

I peek out of the curtains and see the Beards are in their garden. *What are they doing?* They disappear.

I keep looking, but I don't notice anything till 6:42 p.m. when I see Dale and Shaza taking Bizmo out.

Moments later, Dale and Shaza are getting into their van, and I THINK I SEE Brendan. His evil face appears at the window by his door for one second. Then he goes.

But I couldn't be quite sure. It's not easy running a two-man stakeout when one of you has badly sprained his leg, and the other is a dog. Wilkins is sleeping. Sprawled on his back, he is snoring like a pirate.

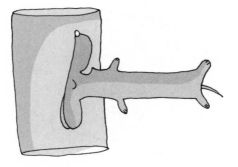

I decide to join him for a moment.

But then I wake up a few minutes later to find *the Cat is in my room*. She is sitting on the floor playing with Wilkins.

She's making him walk on his back legs.

He looks like a little old man (with a very long nose). On each step he farts. *Blll-blll-blll*.

"This is *hilarious!*" she says. "I've got to take him outside to show this to everyone!"

So now I'm thinking: *You've just gotten here. Why would you go straight out again?*

I say, "I don't think you should take him, actually, because Mrs. Welkin says I am looking after him."

But Cassidy must know Mrs. Welkin is in the house.

She shouts . . .

"Mrs. Welkin, can I take Wilkins outside for a few minutes so he can show off his tricks to my friends?"

I can't *believe* that. As I look at her the

cannonballs are *booming* in my head.

I'm thinking . . .

*I said she can't*

*take him . . . !*

*How DARE she ask*

*Mrs. Welkin?*

I'm thinking . . .

WHO are her
so-called
friends?!

I'm thinking . . .

I bet it's
the Beards!

I'm thinking . . . *Bring those jockeys to me. I shall FLING them into space!!*

But Mrs. Welkin is probably just
thinking that Captain Wilkins has been
in my room all afternoon; he must need
a poo.

She's not wrong. Captain Wilkins is now so full of gas he could blast off into space with just his own fart.

"You can only have Wilkins for FIVE MINUTES," I tell Cat. "Clean up after him with a plastic bag. And don't take your eyes off him *for even one second*."

*She* then gives me a *don't-be-an-idiot* look, as if *I* were the one who's maybe about to make a very bad mistake.

"I won't!" she says, and she goes.

I don't like this one bit. But there's nothing I can do. So I just read about Napoleon.

## CHAPTER SIX
### Betrayal

In this chapter, the British catch Napoleon and say he can't be emperor anymore.

They make Louis king of France instead, and banish Napoleon to a small island called Elba.

Napoleon is *furious*. He wants to complain. Then he gets a better idea.

He just *escapes*.

Napoleon gets in a boat, and he sails to France.

BUT THEN . . . King Louis sends a huge army of French soldiers to stop Napoleon.

And Napoleon just gets off his horse.

And he pulls off his hat, and he says:

*"Here I am, kill me if you wish!"*

But then the huge army of French soldiers all shout, *"Long live the emperor!"* and then they ALL march back to Paris with Napoleon in charge—*doom-der-dum, doom-der-dummmm.*

*I AM LOVING THIS!* I am wanting to *march* out of my room, and I am wanting to hold down my brother, so I can pull out his four disgusting hairs.

(But I don't! Give me credit! I don't!)

And then, *fifty-four minutes* after leaving
my room, the Cat comes back. And this is
how I know I am a detective . . .

I am listening as she comes in the
front door, and just by the sound of her I
SUSPECT something BAD has happened.
She comes slowly up the stairs.

Then I just see her pale face coming around the door, and immediately I KNOW something TERRIBLE has happened.

"Have you got Wilkins?" she says.

*Oh God, this is what I feared.* Right away it's like my heart's dropped down a deep, deep well.

I say, "No!"

"I hoped maybe someone had brought him back to you!" she says.

I say, "No!" I feel so weak and dizzy,
it's as if the whole world's gone white.

"I just left him outside the store for *ten
seconds* with Michael and Rupert Beard,"
she says, "while I bought a lollipop. And
when I came out he was gone."

Then for a moment I'm thinking:

*Wilkins has been stolen. I could cry, but I do*

*not want to cry.*

Then I am hit by a volcano blast of hot fury.

"How do you KNOW," I growl, "that Rupert Beard didn't take him?"

"He came into the store to buy Frazzles."

"Then maybe Michael Beard got him!" I say.

"I don't think that's likely!" she replies.

"You know *nothing* about the Beards!"
I say. "They are *evil* and *greedy* and Wilkins is *valuable*! They could be about to sell him. We need to stop them FAST!"

"Look," she says, "we don't know anything about the Beards. We don't know ANYTHING about any of the suspects who might have taken Wilkins."

"Oh, but we *do*!" I say.

"What do you mean?" she says.

"Because while *some* people have been outside, making friends and losing dogs," I say, "others have been getting EVIDENCE."

And I just slam down the five-house diagram.

I can tell she's impressed.

I can tell she is also *curious*. She's been trying to keep away from detectiving because of my mom. But now I see she wants to help me *crack the case*.

"Mr. Detective," she says. "Good work!"

And so now I am still very worried
and angry because Wilkins is lost.
But I can't help but feel a little happy,
because . . .

 . . . *the Great Crime-fighting Duo are*
*BACK TOGETHER!*

## CHAPTER SEVEN
## The Cat's on the Case

"Well," she says, "you can cross off a
couple of the suspects *right away*."

"Who?" I say.

"Mrs. Crompton," she says.

"Agreed," I say.

"And also the Dog Lady," she says. "I saw her earlier. She'd just lost her two Yorkshire terriers!"

"Nicki Minaj and Ed Sheeran?!"

"*Exactly!*" says Cat. "She was crying."

"I am 99 percent sure that it's Brendan. I saw him out there with a cage. I say we call the police."

And suddenly Cat wheels around. "I'm telling you, Rory," she says. "*DON'T* be talking to the police!"

"*WHY?*"

"We are detectives. We don't *need* them. They'll just ask loads of questions and not DO anything, and we need to hurry. I'll sort it out myself."

Is this true?

"What will you do?"
I say.

She *ignores* me. She
just steps right out of
my bedroom window.

Ten seconds later, she is standing on
the little porch roof below my window,
checking out the suspects' houses.

"I'll check on the Beards first," she says. "I'll check on Mrs. Crompton and the empty apartments too. Then I'll go to Brendan's van. I can see his window's open. And I can check Dale and Shaza's too."

"*They* went out an hour ago!" I tell her.

"Did they?" she says.

She looks outside. "And *they* left their bathroom window open," she says, smiling.

"What will you do?" I say, horrified.

"Well, it was me who lost Wilkins," she says. "I could just go in, so quick, and check to see if he's there!"

I am thinking: *I definitely DON'T think you should be climbing in through people's windows.* But then I think: *Wilkins could be waiting at one, hoping someone will come.*

I say nothing.

I just watch, astonished, as the Cat

heads out to investigate.

She does not hang about.

She stretches down to the wall.

She leaps to the ground.

She springs into the tree.

On the trampoline. *Boing*.

Eight seconds later I cannot believe it—she is just walking along the wall.

I watch as she moves swiftly to the Beards' back garden. She drops silently down. She flits like a shadow into their alleyway.

Ten seconds later . . .

I can see her inside the Beards' house.

I can see the Beards.

They look *terrifying*. Suddenly I
feel SURE they COULD be the actual
criminals! They're *definitely* evil!

I've only been around there once, when I was in kindergarten. Michael Beard *locked me in his cellar*, and said I was his *prisoner.*

I see it . . . *That's where the dogs will be right now!*

I'm thinking: *That's where the Cat will be!*

I'm thinking: *They'll be tying her up now, beside four crates of dogs that they're holding, ready to sell, so they can get cash for bikes and stupid jockey gear . . .*

But then I see the Cat is *not* at the Beards at all.

I see her
appearing in
the alleyway
by Dale and
Shaza's house.

She knocks on
their door.

Normally
when someone
knocks Bizmo
barks so loudly
the whole street
can hear. Now
their house is
silent. I can tell
they're out.

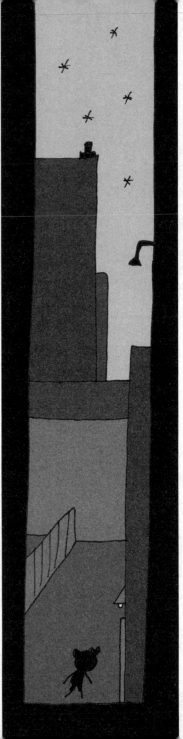

Even so, I watch—*horrified*—as Cat leaps up, sticks her head through the window, then slides herself through.

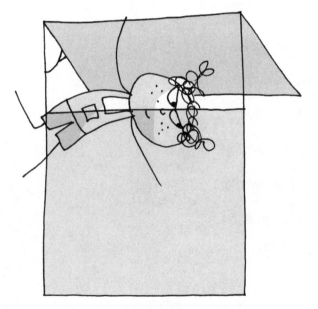

She disappears.

After that
it's a bit like
when you see
a duck dive
underwater,
and it seems to
disappear for
*far too long*, and
you're worrying if
the duck can breathe,
or if it's been *torn to pieces*
by an eel.

It's like that, but about ten times worse.

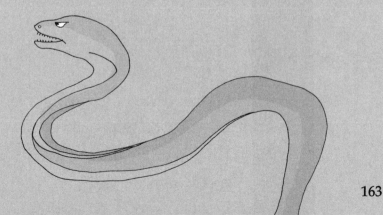

Then suddenly Cat *reappears* through their front door . . .

. . . and I realize I've been holding my breath. I am so dizzy with relief I just flop back on my bed.

About sixteen seconds later, she climbs through my window. I can't believe it. She's hardly out of breath.

I look at her a moment.

She looks at me. She looks like the cattiest Accomplice in the world.

"How did you even get into the Beards'?" I ask.

"I just told them I was looking for the dog thief," she replies.

"Were they interested?"

"Of course," she says. "They've lost Steve, their greyhound."

*"Have they?"* I ask. "So I'd say that writes them off!"

"I'd say it does," she replies. "Mrs. Beard was bawling. So was Michael."

"Then I went to Dale and Shaza's," says Cat.

"I know," I say. "I saw. I could not believe my eyes. Were you scared?"

"A little," she admits.

"What happened?"

Cat shrugs. "I checked the bedroom, the bathroom, and the kitchen," she says, "but I couldn't find anything odd."

"What about the *cellar*?" I ask.

She says: "*What? Where is* that?"

I see I'm going to have to draw her a map.

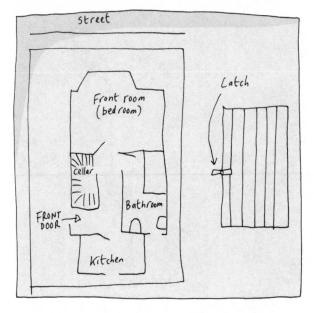

"That's where the cellar is," I tell her, while drawing a big arrow. I also draw a picture of the kind of latch that's on the cellar door.

"Oh my God," she says. "I did see a door like that!"

"Well, *that's* where the dogs would be!"
I tell her.

"Why?" says Cat.

"*Because of the barking!* I can't *believe*
you didn't check it! I think you need to
go again!"

The Cat says nothing.

She just heads off once again out of the window.

Off the wall.

To the ground.

Into the tree.

Trampoline.

And ten seconds later I am holding my breath once again, while she is climbing back inside.

And using my detective imagination, which—*excuse me, Mom, DOES actually think of other people!*—I am *imagining* her as she . . .

. . . climbs down onto the sink (trying not to step on the soap).

I can clearly imagine her sneaking
down the corridor.

She finds the cellar door with the latch.

I see her creeping down those dark steps, and I am thinking: *But* WHAT *is she seeing at the bottom?*

Then nothing happens. It's like when you're watching the duck that has been underwater far too long, and now you just KNOW a BIG UNDERWATER FIGHT is going on.

Meanwhile, I am staring at Dale and Shaza's apartment, and I am thinking: *Please, please, please, please, please do NOT come back right now!*

And I am just thinking that WHEN . . .

*Dale and Bizmo come back!!!*

Dale and Bizmo go into the apartment. I don't hear any sounds.

Then . . .

Dale appears in the kitchen. He puts on *Pointless Celebrities*. Through the window I can see the friendly face of Alexander Armstrong. But then Dale shuts the curtains.

But they're still open a crack. I can still just see the TV. I am *guessing* that this means that Dale has NOT found the Cat.

But who knows ? The Cat is so incredibly good at talking her way out of things. For all I know she could be sitting on the sofa right now with Dale and Bizmo.

But I think it's unlikely.

And then I see what is far, far more
likely to have happened . . . *When Dale
came home he found the
cellar door open
and closed it.*

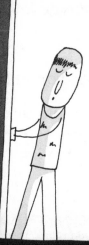

*Oh my God*, I'm thinking, *this is
the* worst *thing that has ever happened!
Cat's trapped in their apartment!*
I am desperate. I am also TERRIFIED.

And it's just then that my door opens,

and a HUGE DARK SHAPE appears.

I scream.

## CHAPTER EIGHT
## A Huge Dark Shape

Then Mom turns on my light.

"Rory," she says, "Detective Maysmith has kindly dropped by to see if you're OK."

The big man smiles. He waves a box of cookies at me.

I haven't actually seen the police detective since the night Cat and I took down the poisoners.

"Are you OK?" he says.

He means my leg.

"I'm fine," I tell him. "I just have my leg in this surgical boot."

He says nothing. I'm thinking: *Shall I tell him about Cat? She did say NEVER to speak to the police!*

I'm thinking: *But that was before she was trapped.*

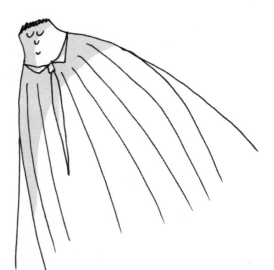

"Mr. Maysmith," I say, "you need to go to the apartment at the bottom of our garden right now!"

"Why?" he says.

"Because that's where the dog thieves are!"

Stephen Maysmith gives me a very serious look.

"What evidence do you have for that statement?" he asks.

"Earlier," I say, "I saw a long, low dog being led off by a suspicious individual in black."

"Did you see the person's face?" says Maysmith.

"No," I tell him.

I can tell I have not convinced him to go to Dale's apartment.

So I tell him a lie. "But then about a minute later I saw them taking the dog into that apartment." I point clearly to Dale and Shaza's.

"Are you a hundred percent sure the dogs are in that apartment?" he asks.

*"No,"* I want to tell him. *"I am 99 percent sure the dogs are in the apartment of Brendan O'Gooley, but . . . right now I NEED you to go to Dale's, so you can get Cat!"*

But I don't say any of that.
And anyway he's not looking at me.

He starts checking his phone.

"I don't think there's anyone with
a criminal record in that apartment,"
he says.

But that's the trouble with grown-
ups. They are always looking down into
their phones, as if their phones lead to a
library as big as a palace that contains all
information . . .

But meanwhile Maysmith doesn't
actually look out of the window. I do.
And . . .

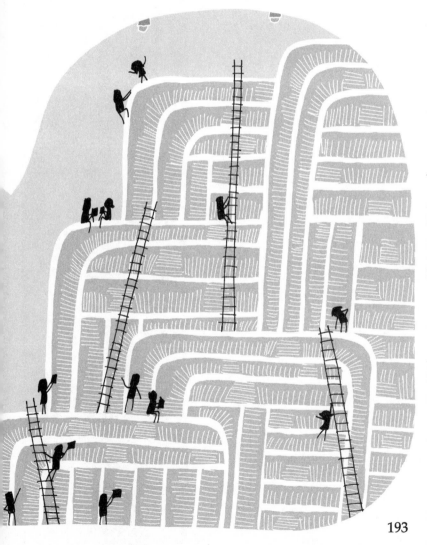

*I now see Shaza coming back.*

And that means she *could* be going to the cellar right now, and she *could* be about to find the Cat, who will end up stuffed, on a wall.

"Mr. Maysmith," I say, "please go there right *now*. And also stop in at Brendan's next door. I think he's helping them. I saw him with a dog cage."

The police detective just stares at me.

"Oh, Rory, Rory," he says, smiling fondly. "The days have *long* passed since police officers could go busting into houses based on the obscure tip-off of a young boy . . . These days we need warrants, forms, *evidence*."

I can't believe it. I see he's not going to go. So then I do what they tell you to do at school . . .

I tell the truth.

"Mrs. Welkin's dog, Wilkins, has been taken," I tell him. "And I think that Cassidy has gone to Dale's apartment to find him . . ."

(I do say: I *think* Cassidy has gone over there . . . So I still might not get in trouble for sending her.)

"Well," says Maysmith, "I certainly HOPE she has not. Because that would be a very SERIOUS offense."

He doesn't seem to have taken in that Cat's *in* that apartment. I can't think how to make him go. I think I might cry.

"Oh, Rory," he says fondly.

And just from his face I can see that he's about to tell me some long, boring story, and I think, if he does, my head will explode like a bomb.

But it just shows how actually you *should never* judge a book by its cover. Because then Stephen Maysmith tells me the most interesting thing anyone's ever said.

## CHAPTER NINE
## Someone Actually
## Tells Me Something

"I always feel protective toward you,"
says Maysmith. "Because it was me who
actually found you on that day."

"What?"

"On the day your dad ran off," says

Maysmith, "and you were left alone in the car . . . remember? It was *me* who found you."

I just say, "My dad . . . left me alone . . . in a car?"

And as I look into Maysmith's eyes I am realizing he is talking about a very important memory that I had completely forgotten. But I now remember it . . .

I am seeing me and Dad in a car.

Then Dad runs off. *But where did he go?*

As I stare at Maysmith's eyes now I'm thinking: *I cannot believe it*. For the first time I've realized there was a WITNESS on the day when Dad ran off . . .

And it was me.

As Maysmith looks back at me HE is realizing he has said something that he should NOT have.

"Does your mom not talk about this?" he asks.

"No!" I tell him. "She definitely does *not*!"

He looks really uneasy. "Well, probably best not to mention this," he says.

"Anyway, I'm glad to see you're on the mend," he continues, coughing and passing over the cookies. "I'd better get going!"

And he goes.

Moments later, I am looking at my open bedroom door and thinking: *What did he just tell me?*

And one second later I am thinking:
*And if Maysmith won't get Cat, WHO
WILL?* I'm thinking: *Who could I tell?*

I'm thinking: *I could tell Mom. But she
would KILL me.*

I'm thinking: *I can't tell my brother. That
would be like telling Mom.*

*I could tell Mrs. Welkin,* I think.

But then I think that if Mrs. Welkin
went to Dale's, there might be a big
FIGHT . . .

*I could tell Mrs. Welkin,* I'm thinking.

But then I think that, if she went to Dale's door, there might be a big FIGHT to get Cat out of that cellar and past Bizmo. And I'm thinking: *Mrs. Welkin is great if you want someone to make you hot chocolate.*

But I'd say she'd not be much good in a fight.

*If ONLY my dad was here*, I'm thinking.
*I could tell HIM.*

*He'd bang on Dale's door. He'd karate-chop Bizmo . . .*

*Two seconds later, he and Cat would be walking home along the wall being cool . . .*

*But Dad's not here.*

I think it all through, like Napoleon. But the more I think, the more I can only see one possible plan, and I don't like it at all . . .

*I must send myself into battle.*

And I can see *so* many problems with this plan. They start hitting me like cannonballs . . .

I'm thinking . . .

How will I get Dale to open the door?

Corner Boy's cookies!! I'll pretend to be selling them. He'll open up!

But they're DISGUSTING!

Doesn't matter! They took our hedgehog. They DESERVE to eat maggots!

Arming myself with cookies, I head off to war.

But there are still SO many problems,
and the next is my *badly* sprained leg.
Just leaving the room I clunk my surgical
boot against the doorway. It lets loose an
EXPLOSION OF PAIN!

But I'm not scared of a little pain.
I keep going.

As I reach the bottom of the stairs I can see Mrs. Welkin through the living-room door. "Rory," she calls, "*Country Wide* is about to start!" (She knows I LOVE *Country Wide*, because I love watching the badgers and the voles!)

I'd love to be sitting on the sofa watching TV with Mrs. Welkin. But I don't think Napoleon would stop, even for voles. I keep going.

As I go through the kitchen the biggest problem is going BOOM in my head . . .

*BIZMO.*

Even if I can open the cellar door, how will Cat get out without being *KILLED* by the HUGE LETHAL ROTTWEILER?

And I can't think of a solution to that one.

But as I head through the garden
I think of something I learned from
Napoleon . . .

*There's a time to make plans.*
*There's a time to STOP making plans.*
*There's a time for ACTION.*

I figure that time
is now. And I set
off into battle. But
I go in by a way
Napoleon would
never have
gone . . .

I am shuffling on
my bottom, like a little
dog with worms.

As I land in Dale and Shaza's garden I
find a skateboard. *Nice*, I think, and as
I head toward battle on my skateboard I
realize I'm actually feeling GOOD that
I'm going to get my friend back.

For a moment I feel very CONFIDENT.
I pull myself up at Dale's front door and
knock.

Then someone appears in the alleyway
behind me. I yelp.

I turn and I see it's Brendan O'Gooley.

He looks pale and stubbly with mad
round eyes.

*"Can you go away?"*
I want to say. *"I am not ready
to DEAL with you yet. I need to rescue
my Accomplice who is trapped in a cellar!"*

"What are you doing?" he says.

"I'm selling cookies," I tell him. "They're
for dogs!"

Suddenly his face crumples.

"Well, I won't be needing those!" he says. "I lost my Gordon yesterday!"

"Gordon?"

"My dog. Have you seen him?"

"What does he look like?"

"He's a very long dog," says Brendan (trying very hard not to cry), "with short legs."

"Oh," I say. "The furry crocodile!"

"Do you know something?" he asks.

"I saw him being taken away," I tell him, "by someone in a black coat with a black hat. I was too far away to see their face."

"Oh God!" says Brendan, and now he really does cry.

"I've been looking for him ever since he disappeared! At one point I heard a dog had been found, and I went rushing out with his travel cage, but"—at this point Brendan's voice goes all squeaky—"the dog that had been found was *NOT* Gordon!"

As I watch Brendan sob I am thinking: *So that's why he's been so weird! He's lost his dog, and he's been upset!* I'm thinking: *I have spent the last few hours CERTAIN that that man was a criminal. I am actually a terrible detective!*

I'm thinking: *I have gotten NOWHERE at working out who's taking these dogs!*

*For all I know*, **I'm thinking**, *it's my brother who's doing it, because he's jealous of their furry faces. My brother could be with all the stolen dogs right now.*

But I think it's unlikely.

And then, standing in that alleyway,
I realize that, *if* the evil criminal dog thief
is NOT Brendan, there's really only one
other person who it could be . . .
and I've just knocked on
his door.

Dale.

As I look at his
pale face through
the window I am
realizing I have
actually cracked the
case.

I also realize I am in THE DEADLIEST

OF DEADLY DANGERS!!!

229

## CHAPTER TEN
## In the Deadliest
## of Deadly Dangers

Dale opens the door.

"What do you want?" he says.

"I'm selling cookies," I say. "I'm raising money for Mr. Gilligan who is still in the hospital."

"Oh," says Dale. "I don't have any money!"

He's about to close the door. But then I get another idea!

"I've been selling for ages," I say, "and my foot is tired." (I show him the surgical boot.) "Would you like to just *have* the cookies—for your dog?"

"Oh," he says.

He smiles. (He actually looks nicer than you'd expect.)

"That's very nice of you! Bizmo?"

Suddenly Bizmo appears.

Bizmo looks HUGE and SAVAGE and SLOBBERY.

"Bizmo," warns Dale. "Be *nice.*"

I hold out a cookie to Bizmo.

He comes forward. He sniffs it.

For a moment it's like Bizmo is at a top restaurant and he is sniffing to check on ingredients . . .

And then . . .

*Rrrrr-rrrrr-rrrrr*, and he GOBBLES down the cookie. (For a moment my hand is actually INSIDE his big mouth.) Then . . .

. . . he sits. He also gives me a look as if to say: *I am such a very, very, very good boy . . . Now . . . more cookies?*

I turn to Dale. "Should I give him all of them?"

"Er . . . fine," he says. "I'll just . . ."

And he heads into the apartment.

So for a moment I am having a grand old time, being the sweet boy at the door giving the dog the cookies. But all the time I am trying to think of HOW I can get into the house.

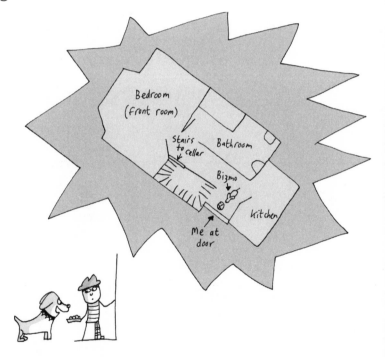

Then suddenly I get an idea.

"Can I come in," I ask Dale, "and use your bathroom?"

"Er," says Dale, thinking. "All right . . . go on."

"Thank you," I say.

And the next moment, I can't believe it:

*I am in their apartment,*
*smelling their stinky*
*smell (a mix of beer,*
*ashtrays, and dog).*

As I hobble down their hall I check the cellar door. There *is* a latch! It IS closed!

I listen carefully. *Can I hear dogs down below?* I am not sure. *Can I hear Cat?*

I am wanting to loosen that latch as I pass, but I am SENSING that behind me Dale is watching.

He is.

"It's the door on your right," he says.

"Thank you," I reply.

"Who are you talking to?" It's Shaza's voice coming from the kitchen.

"Just a boy," answers Dale.

*Just a boy?!* I am thinking. *Just a BOY??!!* Just you WAIT to SEE what I will do! Then I think: *What will I do?* I don't know myself!

For now I go into their bathroom and I wee.

As I do I notice I am splattering the floor, which my mother tells me NEVER to do. *"If you splatter,"* she says, *"wipe with a tissue!"*

I am thinking: *Should I wipe with a tissue?* Then I am thinking: *Hang on, these guys have got Cat, they might have Wilkins, and they DEFINITELY took his hedgehog . . .*

So I pee on their floor—on purpose.

As I do I'm thinking: *When I come out of this bathroom Dale must NOT be watching for me!* (I need him to get bored). So I waste time. I wash my hands. I'm almost tempted to floss my teeth.

And as I leave the bathroom the delay

has worked because . . .

I can just see him through the kitchen door. He's watching TV.

I sneak as lightly as I can across the corridor. I reach the cellar, flip the latch, open the door, then swerve inside fast (leaving the door open just a crack).

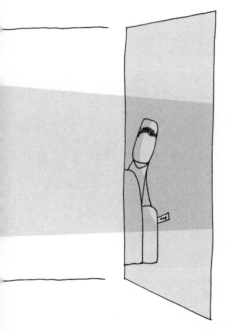

There's someone there.

It's Cat.

She's so close I can feel her warmth. Her head is only about five inches from mine. There's just a crack of light shining on it.

"Hello!" she mouths.

"Hello!" I mouth back. "Is Wilkins there?"

"Rory," she whispers. "We have solved the case! They're *all* down there! It's sound-proofed to hide the noise. But I've heard the people talking through this door. They're definitely selling the dogs to make money."

Just then I hear
a low, dangerous
growl.

Cat actually smiles. (She's like this! The bigger the danger, the more she smiles!)

"We have a small problem," she says. "What do you say we do now?"

"I think *I* might be OK," I say. "I just gave that dog cookies, but you and the other dogs need to avoid him."

"But how will we do that?" she says.

Cat is looking up at me with hope, as if I'm Napoleon about to make a plan. But the trouble is: *I have no plan.*

I think: *I should make one.* And I do.

"Get the dogs ready," I tell her. "Then wait here, holding the door, till you hear a big bang. Then count to twenty, and **RUN.**"

Cat smiles. "How will I know how quickly to count?" she asks.

"You count 'one unicorn,'" I say. "Then 'two unicorns, three unicorns' . . ."

She smiles. "Thank you for coming for me!" she says.

"Oh," I tell her, "you are my Accomplice. If you are caught, I will come for you!"

"*Deadly Branagan,*" she says, "you're the best." She squeezes my hand.

So now I am just wanting to stay in this passageway forever and ever with her, but behind me Bizmo growls again.

He is now sounding even BIGGER and more vicious.

I count one unicorn, two unicorns, three unicorns . . .

Then I push open the door.

In the hallway Bizmo sniffs me. You can tell he thinks it's odd I'm coming from the cellar. But he also remembers I gave him cookies. He doesn't bite.

I look around. No one is watching. Thank God.

Hobbling down the hallway I look toward the kitchen door, and it's now that I see something very surprising.

It's a photo of Dale with someone I recognize—a cool, good-looking man in a leather jacket. I know exactly who THAT is . . .

Dad.

Dale sees me staring.

"How do you know my dad?" I ask him.

He looks at me, amazed.

"Your dad," he says, "is *Padder Branagan*?"

"Yeah, but how do you know him?"
I ask again.

"*Everyone* knows your dad," says
Dale. "He was a two-time World Rally
champion."

"*Was he?!!*" I say.

"Yes!" says Dale. "But I knew him
because he drove for Daredevil Motors,
where I worked."

As I look at Dale I am thinking:
*I actually LIKE this guy. I want to keep
talking to him forever.*

But then Shaza appears.

"What took you so long in that bathroom?" she says, giving me an *evil* look.

"I was just washing my hands," I tell her. "And flossing my teeth."

I shouldn't have added that.

"*What?*" she says.

"It's when you put string between your teeth," I say. "To remove bacteria."

"I KNOW WHAT FLOSSING IS!" screams Shaza. "Get out my house or I'll knock your teeth **RIGHT OUT!**"

As I look up at her I'm seeing I've got this crime completely wrong. *Dale is not the leader of the criminals. Shaza is. She's got Cat, and a whole load of dogs, in her cellar. And if I don't watch out, I'll end up down there too.*

I hurry home.

## CHAPTER ELEVEN
## Reinforcements

And less than two minutes later I am
back in my own kitchen with Mrs.
Welkin. I tell her all about Dale and
Shaza and what we've found. I tell her
my plan to get Cat out.

But before we carry it out I need to give her the bad news.

"Mrs. Welkin," I tell her, "they've got Wilkins."

I can see her going through all the emotions I did. First she goes *still*, then she goes *faint*, then she gets the RAGE.

"Those dirty . . . *THIEVES!*" she growls. "That's the trouble with the world today! It's *full* of hooligans and thieves! *Hooligans and thieves!*"

"Right," says Mrs. Welkin, already stepping out into the garden. "I will go over there. They will give that dog *back*."

"But they have that huge rottweiler," I tell her. "I'm scared he might fight Wilkins!"

"Oh," says Mrs. Welkin, "he WILL fight Wilkins! I know bad dogs like that! (The trouble is Wilkins fights them!) Wilkins thinks he's bigger than he is!"

"But maybe Wilkins will run off?" I suggest.

"But Wilkins is not fast!" says Mrs.
Welkin. "He thinks he is, but he's not!"

"What will we do?"

"We need to LURE that rottweiler out
of the way!" says Mrs. Welkin.

"But how will we do that?" I ask.

Mrs. Welkin thinks a moment. Then
her eyes light up. *She has an idea!*

"Cats!" she says. "We'll make him

chase cats!"

"But how," I ask, "will we make him

chase cats?"

*"Tuna fish sandwiches!"* she declares.

"Do we *have* tuna fish sandwiches?" I ask.

"Oh," says Mrs. Welkin. "We have EIGHT of them!"

"With PICCALILLI!" she roars (as if the piccalilli was the key to the whole thing).

"I shall give you the piccalilli," she says. She hands it over, as if she's handing me a mighty sword.

"And I will need a weapon of my own," says Mrs. Welkin. She goes back into the kitchen.

*What weapon is she getting?* I'm trying to guess. I definitely don't guess right.

Mrs. Welkin comes out of the kitchen.

Mrs. Welkin holds up to the sky . . . a *slipper*.

"Mrs. Welkin," I say, "are you *sure* you want to go over there with that?"

"Oh," says Mrs. Welkin. "I may be an old girl now, but if those thieves come *near* me, they will FIND OUT what I can do with a slipper."

She slaps the slipper on her hand.

I am still worrying whether Mrs. Welkin has got the right weapon, but I can see she is ready for battle.

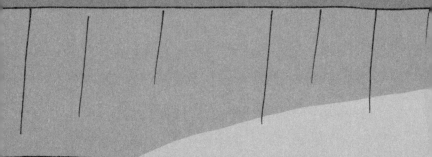

She puts her arm around me.

We're totally together as we head off

to war.

One minute later, I'm in position (outside the thieves' front door on the other side of the wall).

I look

back at

Mrs. Welkin.

It's starting to get

dark now, but the moon

is out and I can see she is

in her battle position.

Standing on the trampoline, beside the tree house tree, she is holding up the slipper and she's as still as a statue in the moonlight.

In front of her, on our garden wall,

she's spread out tuna fish sandwiches.

There is a cat chomping on each one.

"Are the cats ready?" I call.

"Oh," says Mrs. Welkin. "The Cat

Squad is ready."

"And are YOU ready?"

"I was BORN ready," says Mrs. Welkin,

and she slaps her own hand. SLAP.

I figure she's ready.

## CHAPTER TWELVE
## Let Battle Commence!

I count.

*One unicorn, two unicorns, three unicorns*, then . . .

I FLING the piccalilli, as hard as I can, against the thieves' window.

CRASH.

One second later, most of the window's gone and Dale's face is looking out of what's left of it.

I dodge down behind Brendan's wall. I'm just in time.

But behind me . . . Shaza appears with
Bizmo.

"Is someone there?" calls Shaza.

"Come here if you *dare*!" calls Mrs. Welkin.

"Bizmo," says Shaza, **"GET HER!"**

Five seconds later, I peek over the fence.

Bizmo is chasing the cats over the wall.

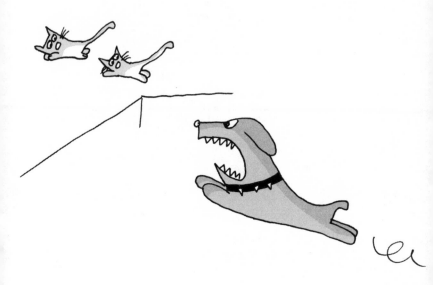

"You dirty THIEF!" roars Mrs. Welkin

in a bloodcurdling scream.

Shaza looks for Mrs. Welkin in the
darkness.

*"You scabby old WITCH!"* she yells.

She *charges*.

But she hasn't seen the skateboard.
She steps on it, then hits the floor with
a SMACK.

Boomtown!

Boomtastic!

I want to see more of the action, but I can't.

I dodge inside Shaza's.

As I hurry to the cellar I notice someone has closed the latch again.

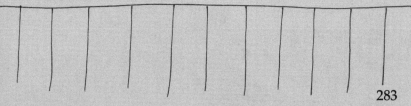

Dale sees me as I'm about to open it.

"You're too late!" I warn him. I

yank open the door and release an

EXPLOSION of dogs.

There's a whippet, then a greyhound, then a big St. Bernard.

Dale is PETRIFIED to see that group. He LEAPS through the kitchen window.

I peek into the cellar in time to see Ed Sheeran and Nicki Minaj, followed by Cat, and, bringing up the rear, like the brave dog he is . . . *Captain Wilkins Welkin.*

We head down the hall to the open front door. Half the dogs have escaped. We're about to.

But now the battle turns . . .

Bizmo appears.

The Dog Squad halts.

"Dogs!" I call. *"Cat! Come back!"*

Cat leads the way. She springs into the bedroom. She's followed by the terriers and Wilkins. I'm the last. I dodge through just in time.

Bizmo hits the door as I slam it shut.

BANG.

Inside the room, Cat dodges over to the window. She pulls a blind out of the way. She tries to pull open the window.

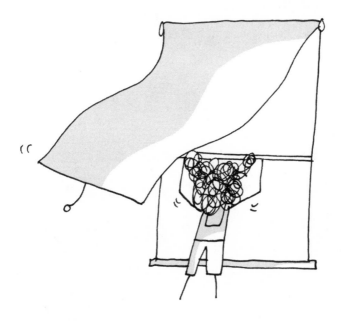

But it's stuck.

I move over to help. And at that moment Bizmo gets the door open.

He can see there're two people and three dogs in the room. He also sees those dogs are small ones that he can CRUSH.

But what he doesn't know is that one of those small dogs is Wilkins Welkin.

And as Mrs. Welkin often says: Wilkins is from a long line of West Kerry dogs who are FAMOUS because they NEVER back down in a fight. And he does NOT back down now.

As Bizmo pounces, Wilkins *springs* UP.

And there's an advantage to being small . . . The small dog gets to the neck quicker!

Wilkins bites.

Bizmo SHAKES.

Wilkins then HITS the floor.

Bizmo SPRINGS for him.

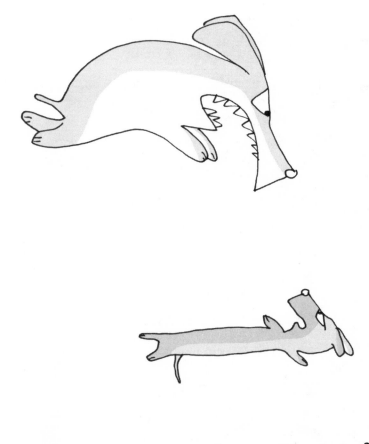

Wilkins commando rolls away from trouble.

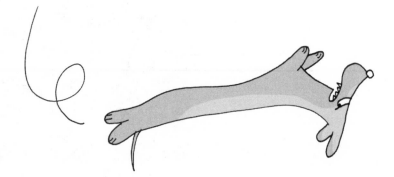

Then he makes a Tactical Retreat under the bed.

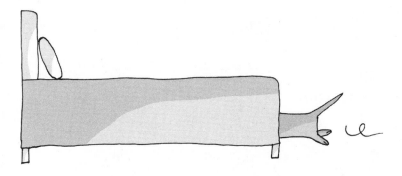

The next bit is classic Guerrilla Warfare.

Bizmo tries to shove his big head under the bed, but he can't reach the small dogs. BOOM! Nicki Minaj *hits* from the side! (Attack from the Flanks!) She bites. She *hides.* Then . . . *BOOM!* Ed Sheeran hits from the other flank. *Sheeran bites.* Sheeran goes WILD! Sheeran hides.

Cat grins. *The whole plan is working brilliantly!*

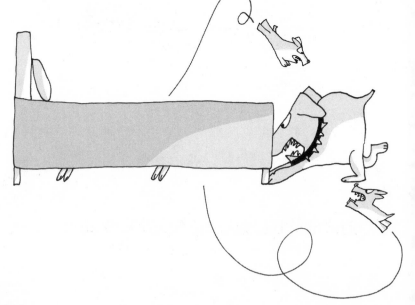

It's like this . . .

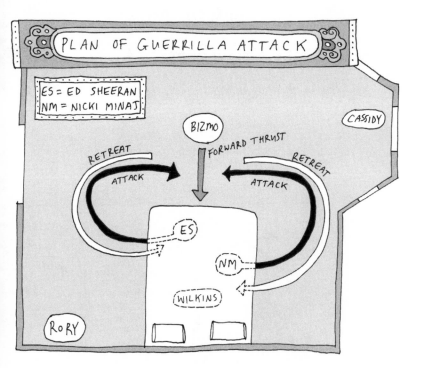

. . . but then the battle *turns again*, as the

enemy's fiercest fighter enters the field . . .

Shaza. She's holding the skateboard like a club. She looks at Bizmo being *wasted* by the terriers. (Ed Sheeran's gone BERSERK! He's got Bizmo by the ears and he's *shake-shake-shaking*!!)

Shaza thwacks Bizmo.

*"Get him!"* she shouts, and she points the dog at me.

But I'm ready for him. While the Dog Squad have been doing their Guerrilla Warfare, I've been *Looting and Pillaging*, and I've now got the weapon that all dogs most fear . . .

. . . the **VACUUM CLEANER!!!**

And as Bizmo comes for me I turn it on

and I BLAST HIM!!!

Oh my God, he LEAPS backward!

In no time at all the enemy is in a

Full-Scale Retreat. It's like this . . .

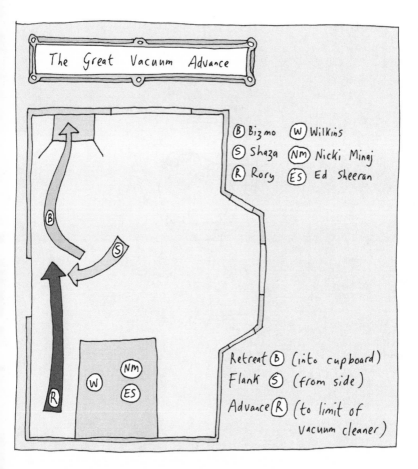

But Shaza swerves past Bizmo.

She then lifts the skateboard. She's about to smash it down on my head.

I don't know what to do. I turn off the vacuum cleaner for a start.

But then Captain Welkin turns.

Has he *heard* something? He has definitely *seen* something. He has definitely seen his *chance*. (You might even say he's been training for this *all his life*!!)

Wilkins runs. He leaps onto the bed.

He SOARS through the air.

Then he grabs the thing he saw, which
was . . .

*A BLIND over the window!!!*

Wilkins knows what to do with blinds. He GRABS it in his mouth, and he falls to the windowsill, going *rrrrr-rrrrr-rrrr.*

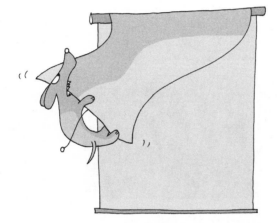

And it's one of those moments when you think there must actually be a god!

As Wilkins releases the blind I see what is almost his worst nightmare: there are *cats* on that front wall.

But behind that wall I see *reinforcements*—good ones, too. I can see Corner Boy, Michael Beard, Rupert Beard, and the Dog Lady with all four remaining members of her Dog Squad.

They're looking through the window.
They're seeing me (with the vacuum
cleaner) . . . Shaza (with the skateboard) . . .
and Bizmo, who's trying to shake off Nicki
Minaj and Ed Sheeran, who've got him
by the ears. (It looks like he's *wearing a hat*
that's *made entirely from dog*.)

"THESE ARE THE THIEVES!" I shout.
And the Beards don't need telling
twice to join a fight. Those jockeys leap,
*screaming*, across the front wall.

*All* the dogs are barking. And I am happy
to say that THIS gets the *attention* of . . .

Stephen Maysmith, the police detective.

He is around the corner taking photographs of the lamppost where the furry crocodile was stolen. He doesn't think anything of the noise at first.

Then he does.

By now the noise is *louder*. The Beards are kicking in the front window: SMASH. The Dog Lady, seeing her Yorkshire terriers, is screaming, *"Oh, my poor babies!"* And Nicki Minaj and Ed Sheeran—leaping out of the window—are being reunited with their owner and they're *howling*, and I swear . . . *those dogs can SING!*

Maysmith comes running.

Inside, Shaza sees the battle's turned.
She *sprints* off down the corridor. Bizmo
follows.

I follow too. And I've chased them as far as the kitchen before I remember my *very* badly sprained leg, and I suddenly have an EXPLOSION OF PAIN . . .

. . . which feels like the Battle of Waterloo is happening inside my foot.

At that moment Stephen Maysmith
enters the scene. He's charging up the
corridor like a hippo behind me.

"Just WHAT is going on in here?" he is
shouting.

*Not much, big feller*, I'm thinking. *The main fighters have left.*

I'm thinking: *I should follow.*

I hurry out.

In the garden, Dale is being pinned against the wall by Gordon and the St. Bernard, and they're barking.

Bizmo is on the floor, *dazed*. And Wilkins Welkin has him by the tail, and he is *SHAKING that tail*, going *rrrr-rrrr-rrrrr*, as if to say: *"I said I'd take you down, and I've taken you DOWN, Bizmo. You are DOWN!"*

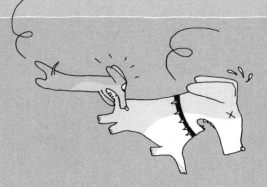

Shaza dodges around the barking dogs. Leaping up onto her garden wall, she thinks she's about to run off.

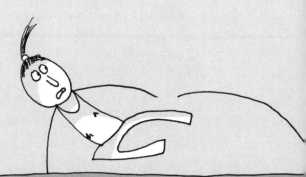

She doesn't know this is the moment Mrs. Welkin has been *waiting* for.

Mrs .Welkin has been waiting by the trampoline like a flamingo by a pond.

"You dirty THIEF!" she calls, then she leaps like a ninja across the trampoline.

 She bounces, then comes down with her slipper going **SLAP**. And I could not say what happens next. (I don't want to get Mrs. Welkin in trouble with the police.) But over the next minute Shaza certainly FINDS OUT what Mrs. Welkin can do with a slipper.

And then I turn and see Stephen Maysmith coming out into the garden, and I see he's about to get the baddies. I also look over Cat's garden wall and see something very important. It's *Mom* appearing in the car.

I think: *If I go NOW, I might make it back to bed before she knows I'm gone.*

I leave the battlefield like I'm a World Rally champion.

## CHAPTER THIRTEEN
## Back at the Base

I am back in my room before Mom enters the house. I am in time to see the police arrest Dale and Shaza in the garden. As they do she looks up at me.

I think: *We took you DOWN!*

I see Cat walking along her own garden wall holding Wilkins in her arms. He's *loving* it! His head's tipped back and he's smiling.

I open my window. "Guys," I whisper.

They both smile up at me.

"You were EPIC!" I tell them.

"I wouldn't use that word," says Mrs. Welkin. "I'd say we were *boomtastic*!"

"I'd just say we were *deadly*," says Cat. "And I was proud to be on our side."

"I'd say the same," I tell them. "But would you mind not telling anyone I was there?"

"All right," says Mrs. Welkin.

"All right, Mr. Detective," says Cat. Then she smiles. Then she winks. Then she goes.

One second later, I hear my mom coming, and I shut the window just in time.

I can see right away Mom is in a very good mood.

"Rory," she says, "what have you been doing?"

As I look back at her I think: *I'd* love *to tell her everything I've done, especially since it proves I* do *think of other people, and I* do *understand about Napoleon, and I* am *a real detective (who can collect evidence and plan).* But I don't.

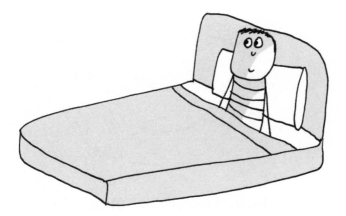

"Well," I tell her, "I don't want to tell you some story!"

My mom gives me a smile that's as wide as the sea.

"Are you OK?" she says.

"Oh," I tell her, "I'm great!"

"I'm your mother," she says. "I LOVE you. That's all you ever need to know."

Then she just LOOKS at me.

I know what that look means. I see she wants to hug me. I see there's nothing I can do about it.

I just let her. She hugs me, and I lie
back like I'm bobbing on a raft on the sea,
and I relax.

"You're a good boy," she says. "Unlike
your brother!"

His BIG
HEAD appears.

"I heard
that!" he
says. He's got
shaving foam
on his top lip so
it looks like he's got
a little white mustache.

Mom and I both crack up.
"What?" says my
brother. "Are you *laughing*
just because I'm shaving? SO
WHAT if I'm *shaving*?"

My mum is shaking as she laughs, but I can tell she doesn't want my brother to see.

"I was only joking!" she calls to my brother.

"Huh!" he says.

"I'd better go and speak to him!" she whispers to me (giving me a kiss). *"Bye!"*

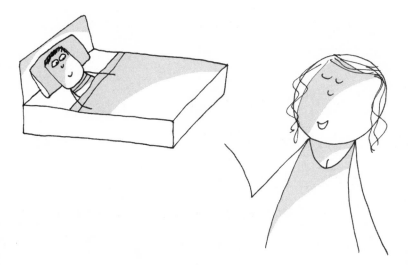

Next Mrs. Welkin appears.

"Mrs. Welkin," I say, "I shall never
judge a book by its cover again! You sure
know how to fight!"

"And you know when to ask for help!"
she says. Her eyes twinkle.

"By the way," she says, "there's a visitor for you."

"Who is it?" I ask (as if I didn't know!).

"He wants to know if he can come in," she says.

"He can," I say.

A moment later, Wilkins's long nose pokes through the door.

"Mrs. Welkin," I say, "do you think he could stay over?"

"I think Wilkins would be *delighted* to stay over," says Mrs. Welkin. "But you both need to sleep or I'll take him home!"

"We definitely will!" I promise.

He is looking at me with his head
cocked to the side.

"Here, boy," I say to Wilkins.
You don't command that dog twice.

Right away Wilkins leaps. His top end soars onto my bed.

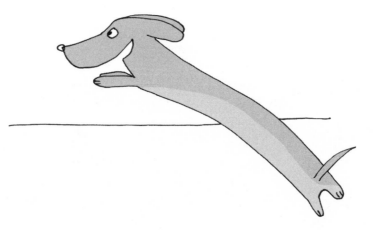

But his bottom end falls short by a good eighteen inches.

Wilkins scrambles up and lies down.
I do too and Mrs. Welkin turns off the
light.

I sniff the fur on Wilkins's head (which smells of cookies). I also smell his fart (which smells of beans). And I think of the battle of the thieves' apartment. I think of Mrs. Welkin with her slipper raised in the moonlight . . .

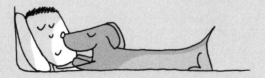

Then I think of Dad. He's driving cars in the World Rally Championship, and crowds are cheering!

Then I think of Dad leaving me in a
car while he runs off. *But where did he go?*
I am thinking. *And will I ever find him?*

But then I think: *I don't care if he's far, far off, across deep, wide seas.*

I feel like Napoleon when they put him on Elba. *I don't care how far I must go,* I am thinking. *I don't care what dangers might lie in the way.*

*I will go with my friends by my side. And we'll find him.*

Then, knowing my friends are close by right now, I fall asleep.

And I dream of cars. I dream of dogs.

I dream of Dad.

*The End*

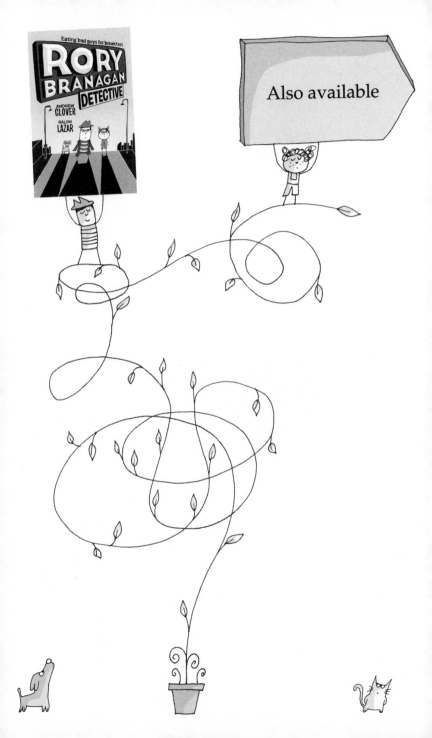

Also available

Eating bad guys for breakfast

RORY BRANAGAN DETECTIVE

ANDREW GLOVER
RALPH LAZAR

I am Rory Branagan. I am actually a detective.

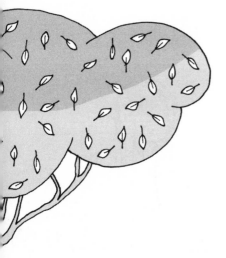

This is my tree house den. It's where I come to read, relax, and *spy on people*.

That is my mom.

That is my brother.

That is Mrs. Welkin, my neighbor,

and—**yes!**—

I *detect* that she is with . . .

# Wilkins Welkin,

her dog,

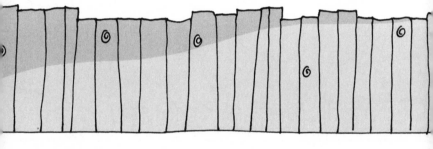

who is probably my best friend in
**the whole world!!**

You might think it's a bit weird having a best friend who's a sausage dog.

But Wilkins comes over most afternoons and usually we go out and mess around with balls in the park.

He's just like a normal best friend.

The only difference is . . .

...he'd never come around on a bike.

And if we're
watching TV,
he only *really*
pays attention . . .

. . . if there's a cat on the screen.

He even comes for sleepovers, and I
don't mind admitting that when he does
Wilkins Welkin and I . . .

. . . we do hug.

As he *dreams* he kicks his little sausage legs, and just *thinking* what Wilkins might be dreaming about makes me smile.

I basically have an amazing life.

But . . . there is just one bad thing
about it, which makes me worry at night,
and that is . . .

# NO ONE TELLS ME ANYTHING!

They don't.

And the thing they definitely don't tell me about is the thing I *most want to know,* which is . . .

*Why did my dad disappear when I was three?*

He did.